Even My Ears Are Smiling

For Emma, Elsie and Emile
M.R.

To Tony Ross and Wendy . . .
couldn't have done it without you!
B.C.

Bloomsbury Publishing, London, Berlin, New York and Sydney

First published in Great Britain in October 2011 by Bloomsbury Publishing Plc
49–51 Bedford Square, London, WC1B 3DP

Text copyright © Michael Rosen 1974, 1977, 1979, 1985, 1990, 1991, 1992 and 2011
Illustrations copyright © Babette Cole 2011
The moral rights of the author and illustrator have been asserted

A CIP catalogue record of this book is available from the British Library

ISBN 978 1 4088 0297 7

Printed in China

1 3 5 7 9 10 8 6 4 2

All papers used by Bloomsbury Publishing are natural, recyclable products made
from wood grown in well-managed forests. The manufacturing processes
conform to the environmental regulations of the country of origin

www.bloomsbury.com

Michael Rosen

Even my Ears Are Smiling

Illustrated by Babette Cole

BLOOMSBURY

LONDON BERLIN NEW YORK SYDNEY

Contents

Welcome

Welcome to our planet.
Please will you record your voice?
You can be quiet or noisy.
It's you who makes the choice.

Later you come to our kitchen.
We put you in a pot of oil.
We look to see what colour you go.
Then we heat you till you boil.

Welcome! Welcome! Welcome!

Introduction Song

I'm going to use my feet today
I don't know who I'll meet today
I'm going to keep the beat today
I'm going to use my feet today

I'm going to use my eyes today
Look out for the lies today
Try to be wise today
I'm going to use my eyes today

I'm going to use my ears today
I'm going to have no fears today
Never mind the tears today
I'm going to use my ears today

I'm going to use my mind today
Leave bad things behind today
See what I can find today
I'm going to use my mind today

I'm going to use what I've got today
How and where and what today
I'm going to use the lot today
I'm going to use what I've got today

Dad's in Bed

Dad's in bed.
Let's squash Dad.
We've got up early.
He's still in bed.
Jump on Dad.
Roll him flat.
Jump jump jump.
Grab his nose
and give it a squeeze.

We're the monkey-monkeys
from monkey-monkey alley.
We're the monkey-monkeys
from monkey-monkey valley.

Dad's in bed.
Grab his cheeks.
Give them a tug.
Sit on his head.
He hasn't moved.
He's lying there,
still as a stone.
Nothing makes him move.
Oh no!
He's slipped his hand
round my arm.
He's giving me

The Grip of the Mummy's Tomb.
The Grip of the Mummy's Tomb.

We're the monkey-monkeys
from monkey-monkey alley.
We're the monkey-monkeys
from monkey-monkey valley.

Jump, monkey, jump.
Monkey jump jump.
We've got to get away from
The Mummy's Grip.
Tickle him, tickle him
make him let go.
Get the cold flannel
out of the sink.
The flannel, the flannel
Splodge him, splodge him
make him let go.

We're the monkey-monkeys
from monkey-monkey alley.
We're the monkey-monkeys
from monkey-monkey valley.

He's let go!
We made the Mummy
let go.
Now let's
get out of here quick

before he turns into
before he turns into
before he turns into . . .
WOLFMAN!!!!!

We're the monkey-monkeys
from monkey-monkey alley.
We're the monkey-monkeys
from monkey-monkey valley.

Late Last Night

Late last night
I lay in bed
driving buses
in my head.

ME: 'Late last night
         I lay in bed.'

GRAN: 'You lay in lead?'
ME: '"In bed," I said.'

GRAN: 'You led your bed?'
ME: 'I said: "I lay".'

GRAN: 'You lay in bed?
         You should have said.'

The Man on the Corner

The man on the corner
with broken glasses
sits on the bench
and watches who passes.

First Bus Trip

After a long, long, long time
of asking,
my mum said that my brother
could take me on a bus
without her or my dad
taking us.

Me and him went upstairs
to the front of the 183.
I sat down as slowly and quietly
as I could
to prove that I wasn't going
to do anything naughty.
At all.
Ever.

The bus started up.
And off we went.

I held on to the bar
in front of me
I held on to the bar
in front of me
I held on to the bar
in front of me.
Even my ears
were smiling.

Going through the Old Photos

Who's that?
That's your Auntie Mabel
And that's me
under the table.

Who's that?
That's Uncle Billy
Who's that?
Me being silly.

Who's that
licking a lolly?
I'm not sure
but I think it's Polly.

Who's that
behind a tree?
I don't know,
I can't see.
Could be you.
Could be me.

Who's that?
Baby Joe
Who's that?
I don't know.

Who's that standing
on his head?
Turn it round.
It's Uncle Ted.

I'm Just Going Out

I'm just going out for a moment.
Why?
To make a cup of tea.
Why?
Because I'm thirsty.
Why?
Because it's hot.
Why?
Because the sun's shining.
Why?
Because it's summer.
Why?
Because that's when it is.
Why?
Why don't you stop saying why?
Why?
Teatime. That's why.
High-time-you-stopped-saying-why-time.
What?

Hear Me

Hear me
Hear me say
It's so hot
So hot
Today

It's so hot
Put on the spray
It's so hot
Put on the spray

Hear me
Hear me
Hear me say
Never ever
Stop the spray

Promise me
Promise me
Now we've begun
You'll let me run
and run and run
Through the spray
All day
Through the spray
All day

Today

Today was not
very warm
not very cold
not very dry
not very wet.

No one round here
went to the moon
or launched a ship
or danced in the street.

No one won a great race
or a big fight.

The crowds weren't out
the bands didn't play.

There were no flags no songs
no cakes no drums
I didn't see any processions
no one gave a speech.

Everyone thought today was ordinary,
busy busy
in out in
hum drummer day
dinner hurry
grind away day.

Nobody knows that today
was the most special day
that has ever ever been.

Ranzo, Reuben Ranzo,
who a week and a year ago was gone
lost
straying starving
under a bus? in the canal?
(the fireman didn't know)
was here, back,
sitting on the step
with his old tongue lolling
his old eyes blinking.

I tell you –
I was so happy
So happy I tell you
I could have grown a tail –
and wagged it.

The Pancake Maker

I'm a three-egg beater
pancake eater;
the pancake maker –
Super Pancaker.

I get my kicks
doing the mix:
eggs and milk
butter and flour;
let it stand
for half an hour.

I'm a three-egg beater
pancake eater;
the pancake maker –
Super Pancaker.

I can flip pancakes in the air.
Oh! It's landed in my hair.

No matter, now it's done.
Anyone here want that one?

No? I'll eat it, fair's fairy.
Eurghhh! My pancake's hairy!

I'm a three-egg beater
pancake eater;
the pancake maker –
Super Pancaker.

Pirate Jim and Pirate Joe

Pirate Jim was very, very greedy.
He wanted to be terribly wealthy.

Ahaaaaaa!

He tried to steal Pirate Joe's treasure
By being terribly stealthy.

Shhhhhh!

Joe caught Jim and flung him in the sea
Now Jim is terribly unhealthy.

Cough-cough! Cough-cough! Cough-cough!

The Demon Manchanda

The two-headed two-body,
the Demon Manchanda
had eyes bigger than his belly.
He walked and talked
right round the world
but every time he opened his mouth
he put his foot in it.

'You're pulling my leg,'
he said to himself.
So he ate his words instead.
I suppose you know the rest:
he went to the window
and threw out his chest.

Pizza

When my three-year-old
has pizza
it starts off OK
but soon
he's got a piece in his hand
and he washes his face with it
he scrubs his shirt with it
he wipes the floor with it
he cleans his mummy with it.

The Angry Hens

The angry hens from Never-when
had a fight and lost their legs.
Now it's hot
where they squat
and they're laying soft-boiled eggs.

I've had this Shirt

I've had this shirt
that's covered in dirt
for years and years and years.

It used to be red
but I wore it in bed
and it went grey
'cos I wore it all day
for years and years and years.

The arms fell off
in the Monday wash
and you can see my vest
through the holes in the chest
for years and years and years.

As my shirt falls apart
I'll keep the bits
in a biscuit tin
on the mantelpiece
for years and years and years.

Down behind the dustbin
I met a dog called Ted.
'Leave me alone,' he said.
'I'm just going to bed.'

Never-ending

5
4
3
2
1 rocket
2 the moon
3 flew it
what 4?
5
4
3
2
1 rocket
2 the moon
3 flew it
what 4?
5
4
3
2
1 rocket
2 the moon
3 flew it
what 4?
5
4
3

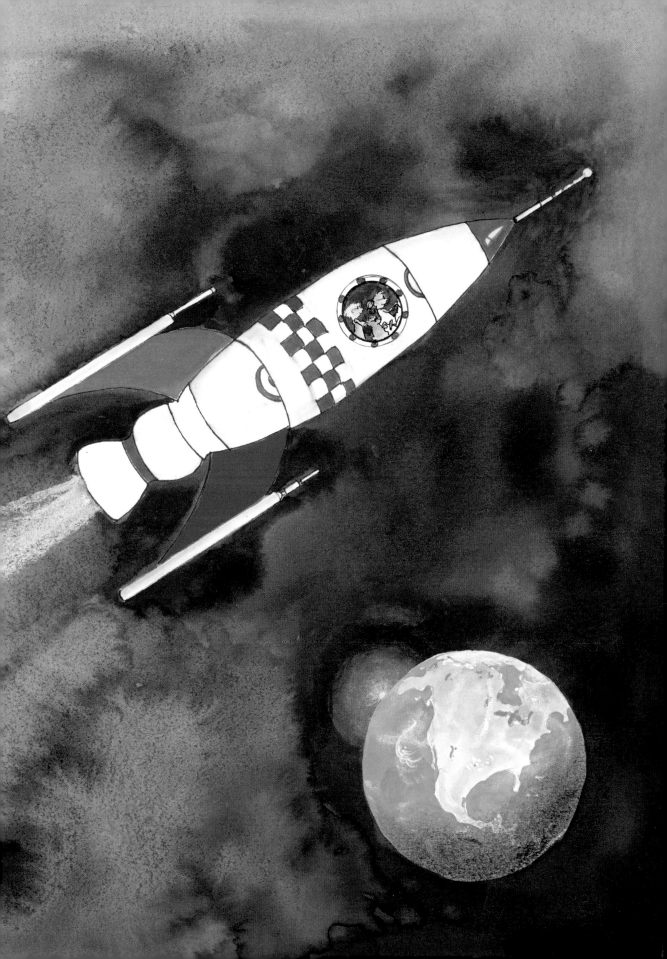

Plastic Bag Tree

The bags are ripe
on the Plastic Bag Tree
Bags as far
as the eye can see.

Apples and pears, peaches and plums;
The fruit is ripe, it's fantastic.
Lemon and lime, bunches of grapes;
and old bags, made of plastic.

Shake the branches
gather the crop.
It's time to take them
down to the shop.

Fresh plastic bags
on sale today.
There's a choice of colour:
black or grey!

Apples and pears, peaches and plums;
The fruit is ripe, it's fantastic.
Lemon and lime, bunches of grapes;
and old bags, made of plastic.

There's plenty on the shelf.
No need to panic.
And next year's bags
might be organic.

The bags are ripe
on the Plastic Bag Tree.
Bags as far
as the eye can see.
Bags of bags
for you and me.

The Child Who Was Wild

Once there was a woman, a young, young woman
She ran from the city, the old, old city
She ran to the woods, the deep dark woods

She wasn't seen for days; many, many days
She came out of the woods, the deep dark woods
She came with a child, a child who was wild.

She brought the child to the city, the old, old city
He grew and he grew; he grew and he grew
His hands grew shoots: green shoots and leaves
His shoulders grew flowers: the lily and the rose
His hair was the blossom, that blows in the wind,
He stood in the city, the old, old city
with the leaves, the flowers and the blossom
falling, falling, falling on grey, grey gravel.

I'm Nothing

Whatever you can't see
That's me
Whatever you can't hear
That's me
Whatever you can't touch
That's me
Whatever you can't taste
That's me
Whatever you can't smell
That's me
Whatever you don't know
That's me
Whatever you can't imagine
That's me
Whatever you can't think
That's me

Now you know who I am

A Dangerous Raisin
(but my daughter Elsie is helpful and saves the day)

A raisin has escaped
from the raisin jar.
It's whooshing across the table
like a shooting star.
Now, it's leaping in the air
like a kangaroo.
'Look out, Dad,
it's coming for YOU!'

(Down behind the dustbin
I met a dog called Felicity.
'It's a bit dark here,' she said.
'They've cut off the electricity.')

Attacked by a Banana

My dad was attacked by a banana.
Yes, my dad was attacked by a banana.
But I should say
he attacked the banana first.

He grabbed it,
peeled it
and munched it up in a moment.
Chomp-chomp gone.

But the banana fought back.

Down in his belly
it grew horns and spines
and charged at the walls holding it in.
It reared and romped,
rampaged and rollocked.

My dad was being attacked by a banana.
He groaned and wailed.
He waved his arm in the air.
He lay down on the floor.
He pleaded for my mum to help him:

'Help, Connie, help!
I'm being attacked by a banana.'
'That's funny,' she said,
'bananas don't usually do that.'

But then we said:
'Dad grabbed it,
peeled it
and munched it up in a moment.
Chomp-chomp gone.'

'Ah well,' she said, 'what do you expect?
If you attack a banana,
a banana will attack you back.
If you attack a banana,
a banana will attack you back.'

A Fly

From the winter wind
a cold fly
came to our window
where we had frozen our noses
and warmed his feet on the glass.

Down behind the dustbin
I met a dog called Roger.
'Do you own this bin?' I said.
'No. I'm only the lodger.'

She Knew Me

A storm blew up from the North,
A force-nine gale, they said.
I was born at one in the morning
with whiskers on my head.

An old woman told me that.
She said that it was true.
Her clothes were all torn.
And she said, 'I know you!'

My Brother

My brother is making a protest about bread.
'Why do we always have wholemeal bread?
You can't spread butter on wholemeal bread.
You try and spread butter on
and it just makes a hole right through the middle.'

He marches out of the room and shouts
across the landing and down the passage.
'It's always the same in this place.
Nothing works.
The volume knob's broken on the radio, you know.
It's been broken for months and months, you know.'

He stamps back into the kitchen,
stares at the loaf of bread and says:
'Wholemeal bread – look at it, look at it.
You put the butter on
and it all rolls up.
You put the butter on
and it all rolls up.'

Scrambled Eggs

We were making scrambled eggs yesterday
and Mum told my brother not to use a fork
as it's a non-stick frying pan,
and he said: I know I know I know
I was the one who put you on to these
non-stick frying pans, you know.
Today he told me that he was the one
who put Mum on to non-stick frying pans.
Everyone interrupts in this house, he says
and he sits in the corner making sheep noises.

Hog-Pig

Hog-pig waits on a mountain
above a valley in the spring.
Hog-pig waits on a mountain
above the valley where he is king.

He could – if he would –
chew up churches and trees
ram his tusks through castle walls
and bite through men-in-armour
like a dog cracking fleas.

Hog-pig could trumpet in the air
and make the valleys roar
or wait up on the mountain
as he's always done before.

Have You Seen?

Have you seen the Hidebehind?
I don't think you will, mind you,
because as you're running through the dark
the Hidebehind's behind you.

Have you seen the Hidebehind?
I don't think you will, mind you,
because every time you look for it
the Hidebehind's behind you.

Zeyde
(My grandad)

When we go over
to Zeyde's
he falls asleep.

While he's asleep
he snores.

When he wakes up
he says,
'Did I snore?
Did I snore?
Did I snore?'

Everybody says, 'No,
you didn't snore.'

Why do we lie to him?

Busy Day

Pop in
pop out
pop over the road
pop out for a walk
pop in for a talk
pop down to the shop
can't stop
got to pop

got to pop?

pop where?
pop what?

well
I've got to
pop round
pop up
pop in to town
pop out and see
pop in for tea
pop down to the shop
can't stop
got to pop

got to pop?

pop where?
pop what?

well
I've got to
pop in
pop out
pop over the road
pop out for a walk
pop in for a talk
pop down to the shop
can't stop
got to pop

got to pop?

pop where?
pop what?

well
I've got to
pop round
pop up . . .

Strawberry Jam

My brother is the world's best
strawberry fisher.
He will find a strawberry
in any jar of strawberry jam
anywhere in the whole world.

From the outside
the jar might look as if
there are just one or two
tiny bits of strawberry in it.
I stick my knife in
and all I pull out is
the strawberry jelly stuff
with no strawberries in it.
But once he gets hold of the jar
he goes dipping with his knife
sliding the knife into the jam
very, very slowly turning it round
prodding, probing, nudging
deep down into the dark red;
and it's not long before
he pulls out a fat strawberry.

There it sits on the end of his knife.
'Look at that,' he says,
'done it again.'
'That's not fair,' I say.
'Mum, look, he's fished out

a strawberry and I don't get any.'
And I have to sit and
watch him slowly open his mouth
gently lifting his slice of toast up
and then see him inching it,
with the fat strawberry sitting on the top,
straight into his mouth.

'Look, Mum, look what he's doing.'

And I hear the mulchy sound inside his mouth
as he munches it up.

Sometimes when Mum isn't looking
he opens his mouth
to show me
the mushed-up toast and strawberry
in there,
sticking to his tongue and teeth.

First Lick

The hardest thing to do in the world
is stand in the hot sun
at the end of a long queue for ice creams
watching all the people who've just bought theirs
coming away from the queue
giving their ice creams their very first lick.

(Down behind the dustbin
I met a dog called Sue.
'What are you doing here?' I said.
'I've got nothing else to do.')

Nursery Rhymes and Hairy Crimes

Hey diddle, diddle,
The cat and the fiddle,
The cow jumped over the moon;
The little dog laughed
To see such fun,
And the dish ran away with the chocolate biscuits.

Simple Simon met a pieman
Going to the fair;
Said Simple Simon to the pieman
'What have you got there?'
Said the pieman to Simple Simon
'I've got a load of pies.'
Said Simple Simon to the pieman
'Ugh – they're all covered in flies.'

Old Mother Hubbard
Went to the cupboard,
To fetch her poor dog a bone;
When she got there
The cupboard was bare
And so the poor dog had a moan.

Hush-a-bye, gravy, on the treetop,
When the wind blows the ladle will rock;
When the bough breaks the ladle will fall,
Down will come gravy, ladle and all.

Yankee Doodle came to town
Riding on a yeti;
He stuck a feather in his cap
And called it fresh spaghetti.

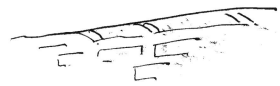

Thirty days hath September,
All the rest I can't remember.

Humpty Dumpty sat on the wall,
Humpty Dumpty had a great fall;
All the king's horses and all the king's men
Trod on him.

Humpty Dumpty went to the moon
on a supersonic spoon.
He took some porridge and a tent
but when he landed
the spoon got bent.
Humpty said,
'I don't care,'
and for all I know
he's still up there.

Little Bo-peep has lost her sheep,
And doesn't know where to find them;
Leave them alone and they'll come home,
Wagging their snails behind them.

This little pig went to market,
This little pig ate some ants,
This little pig went to Sainsbury's,
This little pig went up in a lift,
And this little pig
Went wee wee wee wee wee wee wee,
Oh no, I've wet my pants.

Sing a song of sixpence,
A pocket full of pie;
Four and twenty blackbirds,
Baked in a sty.

When the sty was opened
The birds began to sing;
Wasn't that a dainty fish,
To set before the king?

The king was in his counting house,
Counting out his tummy;
The queen was in the parlour,
Eating bread and bunny.

The maid was in the garden,
Hanging out her nose,
When down came a blackbird
And pecked off her clothes.

51

Wee Willie Winkie runs through the town
With his knickers hanging down.

Baa, baa, black sheep,
Have you any wool?
Yes, sir, yes, sir,
Three bags full;
None for the master,
None for the dame,
And one for the little boy
Who lives down the drain.

Jack and Jill
Went up the hill,
To fetch a pail of water;
Jack fell down,
And broke his crown,
And Jill came underwater.

Mary, Mary, quite contrary,
How does your garden grow?
With silver bells and cockle shells,
And pretty maids all up your nose.

London Bridge is falling down,
Falling down, falling down.
London Bridge is falling down,
My hairy baby.

Three Blind Mice

(The True Story)

Three blind mice
Three blind mice
See how they run
See how they run
They all ran after the farmer's wife
Who cut off their tails
With a carving knife
Did you ever see such a thing
In your life as
Three blind mice?

Now here's the True Story:

OK, it was three blind mice
running after the farmer's wife,
but she didn't cut off their tails
with a carving knife.
She saw them all
side by side.
She didn't run off,
she didn't hide.
She just sat down
with a slice of bread;
said, 'Mice are nice,'
and went to bed.

Tongue-Twisters

(You're supposed to say these three times quickly!)

He tells tea-tales on the see-saw,
The tales that he tells are tea-tales, I'm sure.

He sells tea towels on the see-saw,
The towels that he sells are tea towels, I'm sure.

If he could sell her salt,
I could sell her a salt cellar
for salt for her celery.

I watched a car wash wash a car
I wish I was washed like car washes wash cars.

She said
should she show a soldier
her shoulder?

Here Comes the Robot

Here comes the robot
Bzz Bzz VROOM!
Someone's switched it on
and it's running round the room.

Here comes the robot
Bzz Bzz CRASH!
It's sitting on the table
eating sausage and mash.

Here comes the robot
Bzz Bzz SPLOSH!
It's made the bathroom floor all wet
trying to have a wash.

Here comes the robot
Bzz Bzz BLEEP!
It's sitting in front of the telly
and fallen fast asleep.

(Down behind the dustbin
I met a dog called Anne.
'I'm just off now,' she said,
'to see a dog about a man.')

I Don't Like Custard

I don't like custard
I don't like custard

Sometimes it's lumpy
sometimes it's thick
I don't care what it's like
It always makes me sick.

I don't like custard
I don't like custard

Don't want it on my pie
don't want it on my cake
don't want it on my pudding
don't want it on my plate.

I don't like custard
I don't like custard

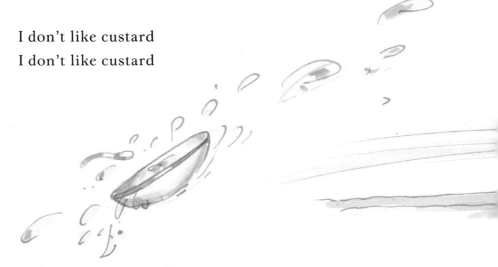

It dribbles on the table
It dribbles on the floor
It sticks to your fingers
Then it sticks to the door.

I don't like custard
I don't like custard

I can't eat it slowly
I can't eat it quick
Anyway I eat it
It always makes me sick.

I don't like custard
I don't like custard.

Cooking Cakes

You know you said I could do some cooking
and you know you said you wouldn't be looking

'cos I wanted to give you a nice surprise
and make a few cakes, make a few pies

but you said, 'OK.' You did say, 'Yes.'
Well, I'm really sorry, but there's a bit of a mess.

I mean to say, in about an hour,
you can use quite a lot of flour.

So don't get angry when you come in the door
but most of the flour is on the floor.

The rolling pin seems to be covered in dirt
and milk has soaked right through my shirt.

A bit of butter has stuck to the chair
though most of it seems to be in my hair.

Yes, I can guess just what you think.
And the raisins. I forgot. They're in the sink.

So I'm really sorry, but I didn't finish the cakes.
Like you say, 'We all make mistakes.'

The Park

Where are you going?
Round the park.
When are you back?
After dark.

Won't you be scared?
What a laugh!
A ghost'll get you.
Don't be daft.

I know where it lives.
No you don't.
And you'll run away.
No I won't.

It got me once.
It didn't . . . did it?
It's all SLIMY.
'Tisn't . . . is it?

Where are you going?
I'm staying at home.
Aren't you going to the park?
Not on my own.

Three Rules

I'm the king
and I can't stand fools.
I'm in charge
and I have three rules:

If you sit on my throne
I give you this threat:
I'll dump you in the river
where you'll get wet.

Don't throw stones
you'll hurt my mum.

Don't jump out the window
you'll hurt your bum.

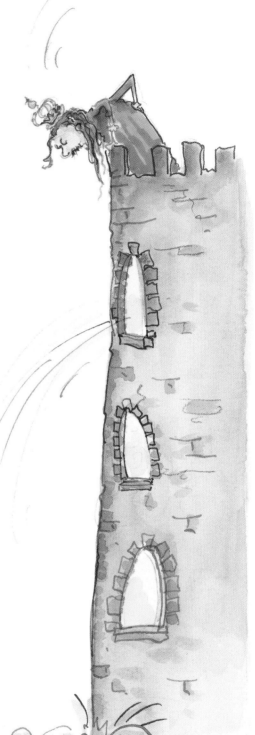

(Down behind the dustbin
I met a dog called Jack.
'Are you going anywhere?' I said.
'No. I'm just coming back.')

Old Ben Brown

The ship in the dock was at the end of its trip
The man on deck was the captain of the ship
The name of the captain was Old Ben Brown
He played the ukulele with his trousers down.

To the Beach

'Rush to the beach
whoopee we're free!
Feel the heat on my feet.
Oh! Here's the sea!'

'I can see it's the sea.
But hey! I'm cool.
I'm running nowhere.
I'm no fool.'

'You think you're cool?
I can see you're not.
Your face is red
and your hands are hot.'

*'I know all that
but d'you know what?
I'm trying to say:
it's cool to be hot.'*

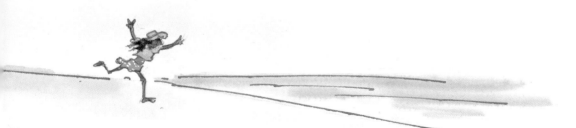

Knees

I'm talking about knees, knobbly knees,
wobbly knees, itchy knees,
bitten by fleas

knees in a scrape, knees with blood on,
knees in jeans, knees with mud on
I'm talking about knees, knees at a dance,
knees in bed, knees in a row,
knees by your head

knees for bending
knees for running
knees for crouching
knees for drumming

knees that creak
knees that kneel
knees that shake
knees that feel

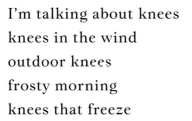

I'm talking about knees
knees in the wind
outdoor knees
frosty morning
knees that freeze

knees under the table
knees in the car
knees in the jam
knees going far

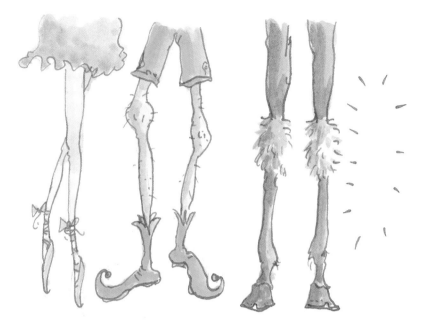

fairy knees
goblin knees
hairy knees
ghost knees

I'm talking about knees, knees on a crab,
knees in trees, knees on an elephant,
little bees' knees

now give those knees a scratch
tickle those tickly knees
then rap out a neat little rhythm
then give those knees a squeeze.

Eating Porridge

Ikey is teaching himself how to eat with a spoon

He grabs a spoon off me
and starts to poke his porridge
poke poke poke
little bits of porridge fly up in the air
little bits of porridge stick to the end of his spoon
he waves the spoon in the air
little bits of porridge fly round the room
he pokes the spoon back in the porridge
there's porridge on the end of the spoon
he bends his head down to meet the spoon
he tries to catch the spoon with his mouth
it goes waving past his nose
the glob of porridge falls on the floor

I bend down and wipe it up
he drops globs of porridge on me

I get tired of waiting for him to eat
I get a spoon and try to feed him
he bangs my spoon with his spoon
he sticks his spoon in his mouth
he locks his teeth round his spoon
I try to pull his spoon out
he grabs my spoon
he starts waving both spoons about
they've both got little bits of porridge on them

I try to get out of the way
he jabs my face with a spoon
he wants to feed me
I don't want cold porridge
he wants me to have it
I duck out of the way
he wants me to have it
he jabs the spoon at my mouth
I let him feed me
cold slimy porridge

I get a spoon up to his mouth
he turns his head
the porridge goes in his ear
I get a spoon up to his mouth
he shuts his mouth
I sing a little song to make him laugh
he grins
I jam the spoon in
he goes on laughing
the porridge falls out again

his tray is covered in porridge
his nose is covered in porridge
his eyes are covered in porridge
his fingers are covered in porridge
I am covered in porridge

DUTTT ! ! !

He tips the bowl up
porridge dribbles down the side of the chair

Ikey is learning how to use a spoon.

A Worm

She's got a worm in her hand
she's got a spider in her bed
a fly went in her ear
and now it's in her head.

The worm creeps and crawls
the spider spins her web
but that little old fly
buzzes round her head.

She rather likes the worm
she rather likes the web
but she doesn't like the fly
buzzing in her head.

(*Down behind the dustbin*
I met a dog called Billy.
'I'm not talking to you,' I said,
'if you're going to be silly.')

Now We Know

Who scratched a Union Jack on the car window?
No one knows who scratched a Union Jack
on the car window.

Who dropped a digestive biscuit down the loo?
No one knows who dropped a digestive biscuit
down the loo.

Who drew on the baby's head?
No one knows who drew on the baby's head.

Was it Naomi?
Was it Joe?
Was it Eddie?
Was it Laura?

Who was it?
Who scratched a Union Jack on the car window?
Who dropped a digestive biscuit down the loo?
Who drew on the baby's head?
Who was it? I wish I knew.

Eddie says it was Joe
Eddie says it was Naomi
Eddie says it was Laura.

Now we all know who it was.

I Made a Robot

I made a robot
out of boxes and cans
with buttons for its eyes
wooden spoons for its hands.

The robot's mouth was a burger box
I painted it all red.
One day I wasn't looking
and it clonked me on the head.

Toys

You'll never get the toy you want
if you nag your dad.
Nagging will annoy him
nagging drives him mad.

What you have to ask for
is a special kind of toy:
a toy your dad can play with
'cos your dad was once a boy.

Christmas is Coming

The figs are in the greengrocer's
Christmas is coming

the silver glass dangly things are up in the supermarket
Christmas is coming

they've put cotton wool snow round the window
of the chemist's
Christmas is coming

there's a band playing 'The First Noel' outside the Odeon
Christmas is coming

I'm a reindeer in the play
Christmas is coming

Dad said, 'I don't know what I'm going to get your mother.'
Christmas is coming

the Beano Annual is in at Mr Iqbal's
Christmas is coming

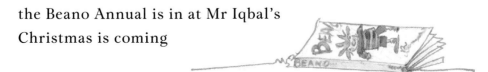

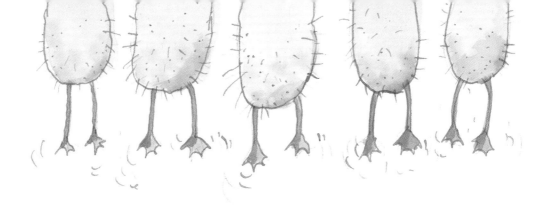

it says, 'Why not order goose this year?' at the butcher's
Christmas is coming

the radio says, 'Send toys to the taxi drivers' appeal for
children in need.'
Christmas is coming

I know what I want
Christmas is coming

I wonder if I'll get it
Christmas is coming

The Zip on my Jacket

The zip on my jacket's broken
I can't do up my zip
my zip's stuck
can anyone hear me?
My zip's broken
the zip on my jacket is stuck.

They say:
it's all right
we can hear you
we can hear you
what's the matter?

My zip's stuck
the zip on my jacket is broken.

They say:
oh
your zip's stuck, is it?
It looks like it's broken.

So I say:
that's what I'm trying to say
what am I going to do now?

They say:
well now
there's nothing much you can do with a broken zip, you know
it's a shame but there you go, nothing lasts for ever
what's done is done, one jacket down the pan, end of story

So I shout:
you're no good
you're all useless and horrible
all the time

I rush out
and I slam the door behind me
very loudly.

I heard them say:
Wow! Did you see that?
And then they started clapping me.

My Tooth

I've lost my tooth down the plughole
it fell out
while I was cleaning my teeth.

It was very wobbly
very very very wobbly
you could put your finger on it
and wibble it round and round.

But it came out
and landed in the sink
with a little PLINK
the tap was running
and now it's gone.

I wish there was a big sucky machine
that I could put down the plughole
to suck it out.

I wish I could have it back
I wanted to put it under my pillow
so that the Tooth Fairy
would come and give me some money.

Mum says we can write the Tooth Fairy a letter:
Dear Tooth Fairy,
sorry I lost my tooth,
but it went down the plughole
if you don't believe me
look in my mouth
at the front on the bottom.

I hope the Tooth Fairy
will read it and bring the money
Mum thinks she will bring it
Dad thinks she won't.

I can't wait till the morning.

Phone Gran

Phone Gran in the van
phone the man with the plan
phone Stan with the pan
phone the fan with the can

phone the DJ with the tea tray
phone the runway that is one-way
phone up my way on the highway
phone the Fun-day about Sunday

phone all the population
phone the people at the station
phone about the operation
phone about the vaccination

you can phone with a moan
you can phone with a groan
you can phone with a phone
you can phone, you can phone, you can phone,
you can phone.

Where are his Glasses?

Dad comes in and says,
Where are my glasses?
I'm sure I put them down in here.
Where are my glasses?
I'm sure they were on the table.
Where are my glasses?
I'm sure I put them on the arm of the chair.
Where are my glasses?
I'm sure I left them by the sink.

Where are my glasses?
I'm sure I left them on the shelf.
Where are my glasses?
Who's moved my glasses?
Has anyone seen my glasses?
I'm sure somebody's moved my glasses.
Oh no.
Ha!
Wait a minute.
They're in my pocket.
I told you that's where they were.

Mum is in the Bathroom

Mum is in the bathroom
and we're camped outside the door.
We're going to stay here
till she comes out
even if it means waiting all day.

We'll get a tent and sleeping bags
and we'll camp out here.
We'll get sandwiches and drinks
and set up a little cooker
so we can have fried egg and beans
right here, outside the bathroom.

Mum's in the bathroom
and we're camping outside the door.
We know she's in there
and we're not leaving
till she comes out.

We'll get a pile of books, paper and pens
a change of clothes and some games
snakes and ladders, and draughts
Chinese chequers and Monopoly.
We're not going.
We're here for ever.

Mum's in the bathroom
and we've camped outside the door.
We're going nowhere.
We're here for ever more.

More Tongue-Twisters

(Say three times quickly!)

Fat flat feet flap
Fat flat feet flip
Fat flat feet flop
Fat flat feet flit.

When Jesse suggested
He'd just digested
His jester's message
He said he'd just jested.

Who done Houdini in?
Dan done Houdini in
Who done Dan in?
I dunno who done Dan in.

Down behind the dustbin
I met a dog called Barry.
He tried to take the bin away
but it was too heavy to carry.

Who Am I?

I'm lost
I'm lost
I don't know where I am
I'm a sock in a washing machine
A strawberry in some jam
I'm a letter in a book
I'm the bubble in some fizz
I'm a pebble on a beach
I'm a question in a quiz
I don't know where you are
You don't know where I is
I don't know how you was
You don't know who I wiz.

So find me
Find me
Ask me who I am
Get me out the washing machine
Fish me out the jam
Open up the book
Let out all the fizz
Let's walk on the beach
And I'll answer your quiz
Then I'll know where you are
You'll know where I is
I'll know how you was
And you'll know who I wiz.

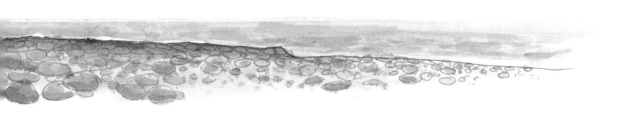

Who Were They?

I've got hands.
They've got paws.
I've got nails.
They've got claws.
My meat's cooked.
Theirs is raw.
I've got a mouth.
They've got jaws.
They're in the zoo.
I saw some.
They looked at me.
They were awe . . . some.

(Down behind the dustbin
I met a dog called Mary.
'I wish I wasn't a dog,' she said.
'I wish I was a canary.')

Doin' The Pig

You can skip, step and scamper
you can jive, jump and jig
you can do the boogie-woogie
but can you do The Pig?

Get down on your hands and knees
put your nose to the ground.
You grunt and squeal, squeal and grunt
and gallop round and round.

You can do
you can do
you can do The Pig

You can do
you can do
do The Big Pink Pig.

A Cow is a Beautiful Bird

A cow is a beautiful bird.
I've often heard it howl.
Owls are beautiful too.
I've often heard them growl.

An orange is a curious man.
I've often seen him frown.
A lemon is a kind of bee.
It's often coloured brown.

(Down behind the dustbin
I met a dog called Nicola.
She looked a bit like an onion
So I thought that I would pickle her.)

Angry

Here comes the man
With the angry dog.

Here comes the dog
With the angry man.

Angry dog
Angry man
Angry man
Angry dog.

Here comes the man
With the angry dog.

Here comes the dog
With the angry man.

David's Book

Now then everyone,
David's had a look.
He says he can't find
his favourite book.
Ah, Matthew thinks
we've got a class crook.
Samantha says
it could be the cook.
David's got some news.
Is it bad or good?
He's found the book.
It was stuck in his hood.

Library

I promise that this is true
you know that I'm not lying
but in the library down the road
all the books are flying.

Round the room they fly
looking for a place to land.
Think of the book you love
and the book will land in your hand.

(Down behind the dustbin
I met a dog called Sophie.
She had won the FA Cup
And was carrying the trophy.)

Don't, Mum!

Mum,
don't lick the corner
of that tissue.

Mum,
don't wipe the corner
of my mouth
with the corner of that tissue
you've been licking.

Mum, don't do it.
Don't do it.
Don't do that
hokey-pokey thing
with the corner of that tissue
you've been licking,
jab-jab-jab
in the corner
of my mouth.

Oh no,
now she's gone and done it.

Duke Luke

He was huge, he was rude.
His name was Luke.
Luke was horrible.
Luke was a duke.

No one liked Luke.
But Luke liked stew.
When Luke wasn't looking
we filled it with glue.

I Promise

I promise, I promise
I didn't eat the pie.
Cross my heart
and hope to die.
I promise, I promise
I didn't eat the pie.

You say you can see
some crumbs on my tie?
And now you're saying
you want to know why?
OK, OK
I did eat the pie.

Arriving at Fidler's Farm

Just as it was getting dark
I think I heard a dog bark.
Mum started to wave her arm . . .
then we saw it: Fidler's farm.

In the night, it was hard
to see the cart in Fidler's yard
but I could see his old parked cars
and up above the barn – the stars.

If

If you bump your head
and you can't stand the pain,
try not to faint –
just get a new brain.

My Bad Left Ear

Dear Doctor, I fear
I have a bad left ear.
It's perfectly all right
with anything near,
but anything far off
I just can't hear.
I'm sure I need pills,
can you give me some?
And, oh yes, in my ear
is some chewing gum.

I'm a Hound

I'm a dog.
I'm a hound.
I run
round and round.
I jump
and I bound.
I snuffle
in the ground.

Watch me run about.
I sniffle with my snout.
I run when we're out.
I come when you shout.

I'm a dog.
I'm a hound.
I run
round and round.
I jump
and I bound.
I snuffle
in the ground.

In

In . . .
the . . .
city . . .
running, running
even at night
in the city
a street.
In the street
a block of flats
empty
empty but for
one flat.
In that flat,
one room
one room lit up.
In that room
one person.
In that person
a heart:
Caboom
Caboom
Caboom.

The Story of It

Sid hid It
Sid did.
It hit Kit.
It bit Kit.
Pat It, Pat.
Pat sat on It.
It ran.
Dan ran.
Stan ran.
Ten men met It.
It met ten men:

Hip Pip
Ill Bill
Slim Jim
Slim Tim
Red Ted
Sad Dad
Slack Jack
Glad Dad
Sick Mick
Quick Mick

Sad Dad had It
Red Ted fed It
Quick Mick, lick It.
Sick Mick, lick It.

116

Ill Bill will.
Hip Pip – trip!

Pip sat on Bill
Bill sat on Jim
Jim sat on Tim.
Tim sat on him.
Red Ted sat on Sad Dad
Sad Dad sat on Slack Jack
Slack Jack sat on Glad Dad
Glad Dad sat on Sick Mick
Sick Mick sat on Quick Mick

Ow!
Wow!

The Olden Days

In olden days
they said, 'Friend or foe?'
And when they were sad
they said, 'O woe!'

A knight didn't walk.
He always rode.
If you wrote a poem,
you called it an 'ode'.

Now here's my ode
it's an ode to my toe:
'O toe, you are sad.
O woe, o woe!'

Love and Hate

I love it when
the wind blows through my hair.
I love it when
I dry my hands with hot air.
I hate it when
we have to walk in pairs.
I hate it when
my mum sends me upstairs.

One Fine Day

One fine day
in the middle of the night
the moon was black
and the sky was white.

I'm always right.
You're always wrong.
If you don't like it,
sing another song.

So, fry my onions
fry my pipe.
I don't like tobacco
and I don't like tripe.

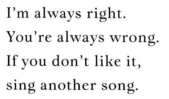